Kindness

Bobby Stevenson

For Sheila

"Today you could be standing next to someone who is trying their best not to fall apart. So, whatever you do today, do it with kindness in your heart."

Front cover photo of Agnes Stevenson. x

GOOD THINGS WILL HAPPEN

Good things will happen

When you least expect it,

They have before and they will again,

It may not be the things you truly wish for,

But when it does – you'll see it's right,

Good things will happen,

When you're looking elsewhere,

They'll grab your heart

And guide you home,

Good things will happen,

I promise –

Trust me,

They have before,

And they will again.

KIND

Be humble, be grateful,

Be loving, be kind,

Be happy, be truthful,

Be caring, be kind,

Be patient, be generous,

Be thankful, be kind,

Don't ruin a heart,

Don't mess with a mind.

IF IT EVER GETS TOO DARK

If it ever gets too dark for you

I'll light a match and let you see

Your first few steps, to get you on your way.

If it ever gets too dark for you

I'll place a candle in the window

From which you can find your way back home.

If it ever gets too dark for you

I'll be the Moon to show you that

It's only shadows that you fear.

If it ever gets too dark for you

I'll be the Sun to warm your eyes

And show you that there's a path ahead

Which will take you where you need.

YOU DO NOT NEED TO BE FIXED

No matter all the nights you lay and wondered
You do not need to be fixed.
No matter all the times they almost broke you
You do not need to be fixed.
No matter all the lies they tried to make you
believe,
You do not need to be fixed.
You and your heart are perfectly made in every
way,
You do not need to be fixed.
The sadness is - that they will never, ever see that.

RETURN TO KINDNESS

When the last kiss to brush your cheek has dried
And the light dust has long since blown to the four
winds
When the last smile to warm your eyes was on a
path
Now long since over grown
When the last hand to grasp your fingers
And help you cross that wild, unforgiving stream,
Has slowly withered and turned to rust
That is when a random act of kindness will grasp
your heart
And pump the heat of belief back into your blood,
And back into your life.

ALL THE FOLKS WE LOSE

All the folks we lose,

And all the chances lost,

The things misunderstood

For which we paid a cost

All the hopes gone dark

And all the loves gone cold,

And all the facts forgotten

And all those faces old

And all the secrets shared

And all the thoughts betrayed

And all the people leaving

And all the hearts that stayed

And yet we wake another day

Inside we have a Sun

To keep us strong in darkened times,

To be here means we've won.

WHEN IT'S TIME FOR YOU TO GO

When it's time for you to go,
Don't turn and wave,
Instead,
Consider this,
If there should be a blessed place,
Beyond,
A land of half-forgotten ghosts,
Then I will follow you and
We shall meet once more,
But if this other Eden,
Should prove unformed,
Remember this,
One day, I too will rest amongst
The longest sleep,
And you,
Alone, no more.

100 YEARS FROM NOW

100 years from now, nothing of this life will be remembered,

Not you, nor I, nor once that we were here,

We only stayed long enough to scratch the sand upon the beach before the

Tide took back its own.

100 years from now, no one will know my name, nor care

That here I stood and lived a life with all those

Other nameless souls,

Yet we knew each other by the joy and sorrow

Trapped inside our eyes

And each of us took that remembrance to our graves.

EVERYONE MATTERS

I remember that day we said goodbye,

The day I asked you if there were any regrets,

You said, you wished you had realised sooner

That everyone matters.

The thing is, I didn't know what you meant then –

But I do now.

Who has any idea how much oxygen a person
brings to your life

Or how much you bring to theirs?

You have no idea why a person is in this life or
yours,

And so what you don't do, is make judgements,

Treat everyone as though they have the potential
to be

Anything or everything,

Love and smile, You are not God.

MISTER BRILLIANT

His real name was Cuthbert Dogoody but to everyone else he was simply known as Mister Brilliant.

He'd never had the easiest of lives, had Cuthbert. When he was five years of age his father ran away to sea – at least that's what his mother had told him – the truth of the matter was that his father moved in with a young blonde lady three streets over, and the man who Cuthbert knew as the postman was actually his dad.

Cuthbert's grandmother, Ethel (the ever ready) was a money-lender who ended up being sent to prison for her particularly difficult ways with her customers. Cuthbert's mother told her son, that his grandmother was spending a few years trying to find the source of the River Nile. It always amazed Cuthbert, later in life, that he had believed the story and had told all the kids in his class at school about Grandma Ethel – the explorer.

His uncle, Stan the Man, who was a part-time magician and someone who Cuthbert had always looked up to (literally, he was six feet seven) died while attempting to hold his breath in a fish tank. The tank was actually in a Chinese restaurant, and Stan had attempted it as part of a bet with Shanghai Lil the owner of the establishment.

Sadie, Uncle Stan's widow, had attempted to fill Stan's rather big shoes (he had also been a part-time clown) by looking after Cuthbert and helping him with his life. This mostly involved Cuthbert going along on dates with Sadie and several gentlemen from the Royal Navy. Stan would sit in the corner of a bar with a cola and a packet of chips, while Sadie sat kissing some man or other.

His best friend in the whole world was Teddy who was in his class in school. Teddy was without doubt the most popular kid in the place. There wasn't anything Teddy couldn't do, or anyone that Teddy couldn't charm. The one thing that Teddy always did was look after his best pal, Cuthbert. No one bullied Cuthbert, not while Teddy was about.

Teddy knew that his best bud's father was actually the postman, but it would never have crossed Teddy's mind to ever say anything that would hurt his pal.

One afternoon on the way home from school, Teddy asked Cuthbert to be his 'blood brother'. They cut their thumbs then mixed their blood together and that was them set for life. At least that's what Cuthbert thought. The truth was that Teddy was taking the long way around to tell his pal, that his mother had met a man who was big in ladies' underwear and that they were moving to somewhere called, Liverpool.

The following Monday, Teddy was gone. When Cuthbert went into school, all the folks who had been charmed by Teddy were ready to bully Cuthbert. It wasn't pleasant, to say the least, but with a little bit of running and keeping one's head down, Cuthbert made it to the end of his school life, relatively intact.

Cuthbert got his first job as a tea-boy in an office of an insurance firm. Cuthbert's duties involved making the tea, coffee (for those of that persuasion), lemonade and a little whisky for Mister McCallister who was partial to that sort of thing.

Everything was going well until Seamus Hooster (of the Hooster Brothers Insurance Agency) got trampled on by a runaway giraffe one wet Tuesday in the High Street. This caused the firm to close and the folks, including Cuthbert, to be all made redundant.

That was the very same day that Cuthbert came home to find that Sadie had moved without leaving a forwarding address. It seemed to Cuthbert that this was the way life worked, for when a soul was down the rest of the world just jumped on top of them and kicked their heads.

Now you might think that all of these shenanigans would have meant the end of Cuthbert Dogoody – but you'd be wrong.

Cuthbert was either not like lesser men, or perhaps he was too naive to see the predicament he was in – but one day, one very early day when Cuthbert had been awake all-night thinking about what to do next – he let out an exclamation of 'A-ha!'. That was all he said: 'A-ha'.

But it was enough, for as far as Cuthbert was concerned, it spoke a million words. At least to him.

For you see, at a very early age, Cuthbert decided that life was difficult for everyone, and people didn't need to be reminded of that. What people did need reminding of was their possibilities. In everyone's life (and Cuthbert was sure he meant everyone) there were bad times, good times, and blooming brilliant times. At some point in the future a brilliant time would come popping up without warning.

So, Cuthbert made it his life's work to remind everyone and anyone that brilliant times were just around the corner.

If he ever met anyone down or tired he'd just talk to them about how, someday soon, brilliant times were just up ahead.

"Not long now," he'd shout to people, and they'd always call back:

"Till when, Mister Brilliant?"

"Till good things come around the corner."

From that day onwards he was known as Mister Brilliant – because (and he was right) good times were just up the road a little, and everyone got their shot at it.

I AM STRONGER THAN YESTERDAY

I am stronger than yesterday

With all its pain and sorrow

And I have made it through another night

I am stronger than yesterday

Each morning I fight to stand and face the sun

Letting it bleach all my dark stains away and

Shouting, Here I am, I exist

I am stronger than yesterday

As I shine a light in every dark corner

Where the Black Dog has left its scent

I am stronger than yesterday

I need to be, because today I have to start all over again

And fight those battles

But I am stronger than yesterday

Because yesterday I won another victory –

I beat the day.

IF ALL THE WORLD

If all the world went dark today,

And the yellow sun no longer shone,

And we felt our paths from place to place,

And loved by voice and words alone,

If we no longer saw our faces,

With all the tales that eyes can tell,

Would you and I remain as lovers,

Or would our hearts grow dark as well.

LOVE & EVERYTHING

H olding
O n to
P ositive
E xpectations

A nd
N ever
D oubting

L ove
O vercomes
V irtually
E verything

WAITING

There's a little house,

Not too far out of town,

Where I'll go when I leave this place,

You'll always find a log fire burning there,

And a light in the window to find your way,

When you eventually stumble over the top of the ridge.

You can sit among friends,

By then you'll be deserving of a seat in the warmth,

You'll have done your bit,

Struggled bravely along the path,

You'll have cried your tears,

And fought your battles,

So come rest a while,

We'll be waiting.

BEING HUMAN

Being human is never really understanding
Being human is loving and hurting at the same time
Being human is hoping and caring, loving and
sharing
Being human is tears and pain and laughter and
fear
Being human is wondering why the hell we're all
here
Being human is being lost for most of your life
Being human is cursing the gods then hoping they
are there
Being human is watching the stars with the same
wonderment we did from the caves
Being human is sacrifice, strength and sometimes
bravery
Being human is selfishness and slavery
Being human is mental illness and confusion
Being human is sometimes an illusion
Being human is watching lovers fade
Being human is regretting all that's left unsaid
Being human is wishing you had done some more
Being human is lifting yourself up from the floor
Being human is writing, painting and scoring a goal
Being human is making music that a heart can be
proud of
Being human is everyone feeling but never always
sharing

Being human is hoping that tomorrow will be
better
Being human is all that we have.

THE ONE YOU HATE

The things you see inside of me

Are never really there,

The things despised, or criticised,

Belong to you, not me.

You cannot see my heart or soul,

Nor why I do the things I do,

You look at me through soiled eyes,

The one you hate,

Is you.

MARTHA'S ROOM

Martha had a room, one that she would refer to as a 'spare room'. Not that the size of her house allowed for such extravagances – she had a kitchen, a little area to sit, a small toilet at the rear of her house, and a little bedroom upstairs. Next to that was Martha's spare room.

When she and Ted first got married, it had been kept ready for a little child. Ted told his wife that he 'wanted' two sons and two daughters, Martha said she would be content with a happy, healthy child.

Ted had painted the walls of the room with characters from books – he had done all this himself in the hope that one day his own child would look up from a cot and smile at the paintings.

In the first two summers of their married lives and with no blessing of a son or daughter, Ted put some of his old books in the room. Martha was understandably upset, but as Ted said, there was nowhere else for them to go.

The years drifted by, and no child was gifted to the couple. Then one quiet May morning, Ted went into the spare room and noticed all the junk covering the walls and floor. He also noticed, sadly, that all the characters he had painted had faded in the sunlight.

"There ain't no child coming, Lord, I can see that now," Ted said quietly to himself, and so, that afternoon, he went out and bought the whitest of white paints and decided to throw out all the junk and re-paint the room.

Ted and Martha never talked about children again, but she was delighted with the new white room which Ted had painted.

"This shall be our room for all the good things," Martha said to Ted.

And that is what it became.

All the presents given to them at Christmas or birthdays were placed in the room in order that they could be admired and kept good. Dishes, cups, paintings, bottles of this and that, were all placed in the spare room to be kept good.

Once in a while, Ted would go into the room and admire all the gifts and would ask Martha whether they could use a plate or a dish, but Martha would always say 'no' and tell him that the room was to keep everything good in their lives and keep those things safe.

When her few friends came back to the house after Ted's funeral, she took down some of the China cups and plates from her room and allowed her guests to use them.

With Ted no longer there, Martha didn't notice her mind beginning to wear away. Sometimes she forgot things; then she forgot names of those who came to call. One morning Martha came down from her bedroom and couldn't remember who she was.

These days Martha looks out of her hospital room window and not far away is her own home with the spare room.

She can see all the good things stored in that room – but Martha doesn't know that it is her house, or that the objects are all the things she and Ted kept for better days.

I HAVE TO LET YOU GO

You'll always be the one I talk to
When I'm lying in the dark,
I'll always hear you laughing,
As the birds sing in the park,
You'll always be my confidant,
And forever read my soul,
But now I know the time is right,
I have to let you go.

LEAVE A LIGHT ON

I will leave the light on for you,

When you find your way out of the dark,

I will leave the door on the latch,

When you finish making your mark

I will leave the light on for you,

To find your warm way home,

I will leave the light on for you,

So, you know,

That your heart's not alone.

KINDNESS

Better days are coming friend,

Just you wait and see

You and I will hug again

As kindness sets us free.

TIME TO BE HAPPY AGAIN

It wasn't the time

For regrets or complaining

It wasn't the time

For 'who'? Why? Or when?

It wasn't the time

To hate or start hurting

But the time

To be happy again.

BE DIFFERENT

Every one of us is made just that little bit different to the next person. It's what makes us all special. Sometimes we are happy with our little special differences and sometimes it can make someone unhappy.

And so, it was with Tommy. Since the day he was born he had what the doctor called, a cleft lip. When he looked in the mirror Tommy felt so very different from his friends. There were times in the village when he saw people staring at his lip. His grandmother used to tell him that no one else was that special and so they passed through unnoticed, but her little grandson, Tommy would always be someone to notice.

But as time went on, Tommy became more and more aware of his differences, and he wanted it all to stop. So, one day in August, he went to his room and stayed there. His mother would have to bring his food to his room and Tommy didn't want to join the rest of his family. He was schooled in his room, and he no longer wanted to go to school.

At night when the moon was full, Tommy would sit at the window and wish with all his heart that he were just like everyone else. And then he would hum a little tune to himself.

Tommy grew big and tall but every night he would still go to the window and sing songs loudly across the valley. It made Tommy feel good and less different.

What Tommy didn't know was that the villagers in the valley below would listen to his signing and they all thought it was the most beautiful music in the world. To the villagers it was the breath of an angel.

The mayor of the village sent out a group of men to find the source of the signing that made everyone so happy, but they failed. They came to Tommy's house, but his mother didn't mention Tommy as she thought that it could never be him and anyway he was always locked up in his room.

Then the day came when his grandmother died and the whole family attended the funeral in the village. Tommy wore a large hat to hide his face, the one that he considered so ugly.

Tommy was very sad as they lowered his grandmother into the ground, so much so that he sang a song for her. He sang loud across the land and all the villagers heard him and they knew this was the boy who gave them so much pleasure.

Tommy continued to sing to stop himself feeling so sad, and as he sung his hat fell from his head.

When he stopped he saw that everyone was looking at him. Tommy started to run for home until the mayor of the village called on Tommy to stop.

The mayor told Tommy that he sang like an angel and that his singing made everyone happy. "It is the goodness of your heart and your soul that makes you sing like an angel. That is your gift from god. That is what makes you different," the mayor said.

Tommy liked this difference and so he continued to sing at night across the valley because he knew that it made the people in the village below happy and that was his gift from god.

He was different, we are all different and those things should be celebrated.

A KINDER LOVE

Even after all these years,
I awoke with you this morning,
Your arms in mine, your heat, your hair,
Your smell, your sleeping smile, your skin,
Your morning eyes,
Oh – those eyes.
Even after all these years,
When neither knows who lived or died,
I can still feel you inside
Clawing at the emptiness of my heart,
I was only ever happy in your company, that much
is true.
Maybe we met a thousand years before,
And swore we'd love in different forms,
Perhaps this time we've only glanced each other's
souls and
Hope the next will be a kinder love.
Even after all these years,
I still dream of you and hope.

BROKEN HEARTS

There's a time in the dark,
When the hearts are parked,
And all troubles will seep through the floor,
In the quietest point of the blackest night,
There will come a reprieve from the roar,
With your face at peace,
And your thoughts standing-still,
And your eyes no longer can weep,
It is then, it is then, that the angels arrive,
To help broken hearts
Fall asleep.

ONCE

Breathe in the sun

And touch the sky

Put a smile on your lips

And a fire in your eye

Drink in this life

And smother the cracks,

For you'll live this day

Only once.

A WET FINGER IN THE SUGAR

I know how long you waited for the days

When all the good things would come tumbling
from the sky,

And on one warm mist covered morning they fell

Not as you imagined, but they were all the greater
for being that.

I know how long you wished for all the kindnesses

To fall into your lap –

Some landed in disguise, but you grew to love
them all the same.

You stuck your wet finger in that sugar

And had a taste of what happiness was

One taste was all that you were allowed and now
you have to say goodbye

But remember this – there are some who never
even got to dip a wet finger in the sugar.

HAS ANYONE SEEN MY HEART

Has anyone seen my heart?

All I did was turn to pick up that drink,

And it was gone.

I left it on the table, only for a second.

I swear.

When I was young, I used to wear it on my sleeve,

That way I knew where it was,

But some of the children at school stole it and used it as a football,

It was kicked and bruised when I got it back.

It always was.

When I was older, I kept it in dark places,

In desks and drawers,

For safe keeping, you understand.

But nothing really grows unless it gets rain and sunshine.

My family would sometimes find it, and ashamed

I would dust it off and take it back.

And for the longest of days, I even forgot it was there,

It was easier that way.

It was stolen a few times, and, once or twice, given away by me

To the wrong people.

So, I keep it close, these days,

Close to my chest.

If you happen to see my heart,

Tell it, I'm sorry I lost it,

And that I'm standing right here,

Waiting.

BULLYING NEVER SLEEPS

There was a man with the large dog who would
watch and wait and make the boy run indoors.
Then the man would smile, chuckle to himself, and
walk off. Every day, that happened. Every day to a
young boy.

Then the boy started going to school and at least
he wouldn't see the man and the dog again. But
there were bigger monsters in the school. Those
who were scared and unhappy and jealous – were
the worst of the bullies, those were the monsters.

When he left to go to college, he thought that his
days as a bully's target were over. But people bully
with words rather than their fists. People bully with
humour. People bully with silence.

When he moved into his first job, he thought now I
am a man, I can stand up for myself. But people
bully with power and people bully with money and
people bully with favours.

People bully about race and sexuality and
disfigurement and illness.

And those who walk a kinder path, those who
should know so much better, bully with their gods.

When he retired he thought that would be the end
of it, there would be no more bullying, surely they

must all be tired by now. But people bully with friendships, in the giving and taking of them. People bully with their time. People bully with loneliness. People bully with the kindest of smiles and the coldest of stares.

Bullying never sleeps.

Ever.

BEAUTIFULLY BROKEN

Sara stepped out the front door with an artificial spring in her step. Whatever happened in life, you had to turn up and shut up; her grandfather had taught her that. Her daughter, Willow, ran down the stairs and caught her mother's hand as they stepped into the world. Sara didn't know, as the two of them walked up the street, that her seven-year-old daughter had lain awake last night listening to her mother sobbing. Willow held her mother's hand even more tightly than she did yesterday.

Across the road in number 17, Eric watched the lovely mother and daughter skip up the street: oh, to be that happy, he thought. Eric waved to his wife as she left to start the first of her four cleaning jobs that day. She had to work all the hours she could now that his hip had grown more painful. He could still climb up to the attic when the house was empty, and those steps were like a stairway to heaven. Up there he could try on the dresses and the high-heel shoes, and in the mirror, he didn't see Eric but the beautiful Titania. What harm was he doing? He felt certain that God would understand.

Helen did what she always did at this time every morning: she would eat her breakfast and watch the world go by from her window. She had stopped putting milk in with the corn flakes and had gone straight to drowning them in vodka. It gave her a warmth and glow that porridge had once done. She knew that by 10am the sun would be shining in her head no matter what the weather was outside. Passing folks would wave at Helen – the smiling happy lady who sat looking from her window at number five.

Kelly smiled at the mirror. She had to get the first smile right. It had to look natural, welcoming, and loving. She didn't want her eyes to give the game away. She had to get it correct, for her sake and for his. He wouldn't be coming home for another week but every spare minute she had, was spent practising that smile. It had been his third tour of duty in Afghanistan when it had happened. She told herself that she had married the man, a brave soul with a good heart and not the legs – the ones he had left in another country.

Sandy walked to the shop to get a newspaper, one that he knew he wouldn't read. Newspapers only sold misery and lies anyway. What was really important was the fact, that if he made it there and back without stepping on a crack in the pavement – then he wasn't a failure, and his wife was wrong.

Katie watched Sandy through her dirty window. She wanted to tell him that he was married to the wrong woman, and that she could love him much better than that wife of his. Somehow Katie's life had passed her by as she had nursed her long-gone mother. It was probably too late to say to Sandy, she thought. Then she heard the voice calling on her again and she wondered if she was going the same way as her mother and grandmother.

Another morning was almost over in the street of the beautifully broken, and up and down the road the silence was almost deafening.

KINDNESS AND LOVE

That first morning,

That breathless beautiful morning,

As the darkness faded and the clouds disappeared,

We took our first careful steps out into the new
world,

To the new normal where the virus had taken
leave,

And only kindness and love had survived.

THE BIRD FEEDER

I am not quite sure when I became aware of her.
Back then, I didn't even know it was a 'her'. She
lived in a run-down cottage on a lane at the edge of
the village.

It was just one of those dwellings that might have a
light on in the room, or it wouldn't. She seemed
never to emerge or indeed look out of her window.

To me, she was an enigma, but to most other folks
in the village, the details of her name or her life
would never pass their lips.

One Spring morning, I happened to be walking past
her house and noticed the first of her birdfeeders –
a little home-made contraption, filled with a tiny
amount of seed. Perhaps it was an unkind
judgement on my part, but from the condition of
her home, I had assumed that she may not have
much money to spend, and that the birdseed was
actually generosity itself.

Some days there would be a little drop of seed, and
on other days the feeder was empty.

One quiet day, I noticed that the feeder had lain
without food for some time. I, therefore,

purchased some seed from the village shop. The birdfeeder was not too far from the lane, and so I was able to lean over the hedge and place the seed on the feeder.

It was then I saw the little old lady smile from her window.

The following weeks I continued to help with the seed when the feeder had stood empty for a time.

In the first days of Autumn, a new feeder hung next to the original. There was a little seed in both of the feeders, and so I added a little of my own to both.

One day near Christmas I added a new feeder. One that allowed the seed to slip down a chute and so last for several days. I wasn't sure if the old lady would object, but when I passed her home just after New Year's Day, the feeder was still in place and still contained some food.

By the following summer, there were now six contraptions in her front garden. The old lady had managed to keep her original one in a little seed, but I would maintain the other five.

In all those years, we never spoke or gave more than a quick smile if she was standing by the window.

One day, a young couple came out of the house. "Are you the man who has placed the birdseed in our Great Aunt's garden?" I said that I was, and then was upset to find out that she had died a few days earlier.
"She left a letter for you – 'To the Bird Feeder Man'."

I passed on my condolences and told them that their aunt and I had never actually met. They informed me that she had kept herself to herself for many years and had rarely ventured from the house. When I got home, I made myself a cup of tea and sat in front of a large roaring fire and read her letter.

'Dear Sir. I wanted to thank you for your kindness in keeping my garden alive with the beautiful birds that visited this village. It has been a struggle with money over the years, and any extra would go to the birdseed. A long, long time ago, I lived in London, and it was during the War that my husband and child met their last sleep at the hands of a bomb dropped on our street. I moved to the country to live with my sister. She sadly passed a few years ago. The little Robins which visited my garden were, to me, my son, George Junior and my husband, George Senior coming to say 'hello'. It helped me through many a hard time. I can only say thank you for your kindness, and that you may

know the comfort and joy you brought to me.
Yours, Sadie."

The family sold the house a while back, but they
left the bird feeders in the garden. I notice that the
new family keep them full of seed.

Maybe Sadie comes to visit from time to time

.

BROKEN BISCUITS

Every time one of us was hurt, or we had our hearts broken, Uncle Peter would always do the same thing. He'd go to the tin with biscuits and take out a Kit Kat or a Twix – snap them in two. Then guess what? He'd shove each half up his nose and chase us around the house.

Uncle Peter was the big bad chocolate monster and believe me when I say it would help. For a few minutes, you'd forget, and inside those few minutes of forgotten worries – was a beautiful release — just enough time to get your breath back and keep fighting.

Sometimes, he'd stick the broken biscuits in his mouth and make them look like extra-long teeth – then he'd be Count Peter, the chocolate vampire.

One day my older sister, Rachel, when she was about twelve years of age, put on my mother's high-heels to go to the local shop to fetch some chocolate digestive. She always wanted to be grown-up. The shop was in the basement of a house on the corner. You had to go down three steps – that was all – three bloody steps. My sister tripped on the way up in the big-lady shoes, bumped her head and was never the same again. She never did get to be a grown-up.

My Uncle Peter stopped breaking biscuits after that day. The ambulance man handed in the broken chocolate digestive biscuits to the house. They lay in the corner for months, until my father worked up the courage to throw them away.

Last month, my Uncle Peter left us all for the big biscuit factory in the sky, and as they brought the coffin through the hall, the congregation stood up and everyone to a man or woman had broken Kit Kats stuck up their noses. I kid you not. Broken biscuits in their nostrils.

I could hear him laughing all the way from up there. Sometimes the simplest things make the biggest differences.

Who would have thought it?

 Broken biscuits.

BE YOU

Laugh
Lie
Scream
Swear
Hope
Love
Screw-up
Be down
Get up
Make mistakes
Be surprised
Be wrong
Be right
Be honest
Sleep all-day
Awake all night
Cheat
Cheated on
Be crazy
Be lazy
Be scared
Be brave
Cry
Joke
Forgive
Forget
Be human
Be you.

DON'T HATE, JUST LOVE

It's a very short life,
And an amazing one,
Full of miracles and caring,
With a universe or two, or maybe more, thrown in,
All decked out with black holes and sunsets,
And yet you chose to spend it hating,
And loathing, and hitting and shouting,
And name calling and abusing.
Whatever this is, it's a short life,
And in your hating,
You've missed the greatest
Experience of your existence,
Don't hate, just love.

THE BOY WHO LOVED TO HANDSTAND

Charlie lived in grey house which stood in a grey
street which weaved its way through a grey town.

He wasn't an unhappy kid – on the contrary,
Charlie saw the world both as beautiful and crazy
at the same time.

But where Charlie was unique was in the way he
looked at the world. He knew that there was more
to life than all this greyness, the question was
where to find it.

His grey school was taught by a grey teacher who
had once shown something other than grey from
her eyes but as Charlie didn't have a word for it, he
decided he must have imagined it.

One day Charlie was busy drawing an elephant, (on
a piece of paper, not actually drawing on an
elephant as that would have been stupid) with his
tongue hanging out of his mouth and as he
scribbled hard, his pencil shot out of his hand and
under his desk.

When Charlie leaned down to get his pencil, two
strange things happened. One – all the blood
rushed to his head and made him feel really dizzy.
Two – the world seemed to take on something
other than grey. He still had no idea what it was

but for the first time Charlie could see the world in colours.

He sat upright just a bit too quickly and nearly made himself sick – but there it was, the world was back to being grey.

Charlie decided to keep this secret to himself and run all the way home. When he got to his bedroom, he had one last look out in the hall, in case the family were nearby then he went into his room and did a handstand against the wall. Sure, enough the world became colourful again, so much nicer than the grey one.

So, every chance he could get, Charlie would stand on his hands and enjoy the way he looked at the world. Okay, so no one else looked at the world the way Charlie did, but he didn't care, in fact he loved being the only one who knew the secret.

One day, when he felt like a walk, Charlie went down to the river and when no one was looking, he stood on his hands and the world seemed right again. That was until a large shadow was cast across his face – he hoped it wasn't the kids from the other street, he knew they'd never understand but it wasn't them. Instead, it was a young girl and what was more surprising was the fact that her face was the right way up.

Charlie was used to seeing a beautiful world but with people the wrong way around.

You see, the pretty young girl loved to see the world the same way as Charlie did. She loved to stand on her hands too and that made Charlie happy.

The two of them could share this beautiful world together.

Charlie was no longer alone.

WRITE OR WRONG

I never really quite belonged,
To anyone or anywhere,
Except the worlds inside my head,
I'm always made so welcome there.

SOMEONE ELSE'S PERFECT

Don't waste your breath,
Being someone else's perfect,
Don't struggle or crawl across
Someone else's winning line,
Make it your own race,
Win or lose, the rules are yours,
Please, please, don't waste your life
Being someone else's perfect,
Breathe in deep, let go and be free.

SHOREHAM VILLAGE'S'S LITTLE SECRET

Most of her 94 years had been spent in this beautiful little corner of the world. The rear of her property looked up to the Cross on the hill above, and now that most of her days were spent with resting in bed – she found this a favourable view. In the Spring and the Summer months, she watched the little birds and then the wild geese as they came to visit in her back yard and the fields beyond.

It hadn't always been this way. In her younger, vibrant days she had worked on the farm, and later in the Cooperative shop on the village High Street. She had been born into a place that had meant the most happiness and therefore, had never wanted to leave. She had been married for a short time, there had been no children, but she had accepted that fact and moved on with her life. Her husband had always wanted sons and daughters and had eventually found a family with his second wife, in Hastings.

In all her 94 years much of it had been spent looking from her window on to the passers-by and their changing tastes and fashions - and as the older residents had aged and passed on, so the village constantly invigorated itself with newer, younger dynamic families. Most of these folks now worked in the city, and as such spent much of their time commuting. She had been lucky. She had found everything she needed within reach. Not many had had that chance.

But the main thing that preoccupied her thoughts was the magic in this little haven. Her great grandmother, a woman who had been there at the opening of the Co-op shop - in the same year that Queen Victoria had died – had always told her the same sentence over and over again, 'Shoreham finds you, you don't find Shoreham'.

She had always wondered what that had meant – but it wasn't about the likes of herself or her family, it was about the souls who thought they had discovered this hamlet by accident - a lucky accident – but an accident all the same.

Yet she knew the truth. They came here incomplete, or sad, or single, or unhappily married, or sick, or healthy, or hopeful, or lost – and they stayed long enough to put things right in their lives.

To find that special person, or to lose the wrong one. To beat the depression or some disease or another. To raise a family or find a new one. To see the end of loneliness in the company of new friends, or to find a confidence when it was lacking.

Whatever their needs, Shoreham grabbed them as they passed by, then dusted them down and didn't let go until the time was right for them to move on. She had seen it time and time again – enough to know that it wasn't a fluke but a certainty - a miracle.

It was a truth that not everyone came to the village searching for something, but most of them did. They just didn't know it.

And from her little window on the High Street, she had watched them find it and had taken comfort in their happiness, and their newfound lives.

Now from her bedroom window, she watched as the geese came to the field beyond the trees. Those beautiful birds waited on her to close her eyes for the very last time, and then they carried her soul, to that far country where she could rest.

(To all those who found it.)

IN SOME OTHER LIVES

If only they had talked, or smiled, or laughed,

They would have known,

They were meant for one another,

Matching souls.

The Universe had worked its magic to get them this close,

But they didn't look up, or across,

And so, the chance was gone forever,

Or at least until they met again,

In some other lives.

LOVE AND HOPE

You asked me, my young one, as we sat by the sea

What life had brought to my heart.

"Was it joy, was it sadness,

Was it laughter and tears?

The kindness of lovers?

The friendship through years?

Or the dreams of a life

In a heaven above?"

"It was none of these things,

It was hope,

It was love."

WHEN I RISE

When I rise, it won't be phoenix like from the ashes,

Instead it will be me, myself, scrambling and climbing up the healed scars

Which sit upon my back.

When I rise, it will because of the winds that take me there

When I rise, it will be with imagination and kindness,

And not by standing upon the shoulders of others.

YOU'RE OKAY

Stop confusing, abusing and using -
The one that you see in the glass
Stop berating, deflating, and hating -
That soul which you treat as an ass
Stop telling and dwelling on matters that sadden
Stop blaming and shaming a heart
Make it harden
Stop knocking yourself to folks near and far
Stop saying you're sorry
For the person you are.

You're okay.

Seriously.

WHISPERS

I know all of this is crazy
Every last crazy second of it
And I know that there have been bad times
And good times, and times that it hurts so bad that
You feel as if your heart has stopped.
But there has been laughter too, and friendship
And all the silent victories.
And love, most importantly, love.
No matter what form it's taken.
So yeh, I know it's crazy,
What with all of this going on and no reason for
any of it,
But I'm going give it a try for another day
Just to see what happens.

THE CLOUD CLIMBER

Stan had a brilliant job, one that many people would have given their back teeth to have. People were always telling him – "that's the kind of job I'd like to have Stan." Stan would just smile and move on.

Ever since he was a kid, Stan had always wanted to be a cloud-climber. "That's pie in the sky," folks would say. "Your head's in the clouds," and Stan would just keep quiet and move on.

Stan would get up at 2am every night, when the house was sleeping and by candlelight he would take out his books on cloud-climbing and study until the morning light broke through the window.

Then the day came when Stan told his family and friends that he was leaving his job to become a cloud-climber. His family thought he must be ill because no one in the family had ever been a cloud climber. "I'm sorry," he said, "that you feel that way, but it is what I was born to do."

"Nonsense," said his friends. "How stupid," said his aunts and uncles. "The boy must be mad," said his old teacher.

Then came the day when Stan got to climb his first cloud. After a hard day's work, he arrived at the top of the cloud where he breathed in the sweetest of all the airs, and where the sun warmed his contented face.

Up here he knew he was at home and that no one could tell him that he wasn't born to climb clouds.

Stan, the cloud climber, just smiled because right there and then he knew he was special.

He finally understood what it felt like to do what you had been born to do - and not everyone knew how that felt.

THE HEART OF A DYING STAR

There was a moon that night,
That shook my comfortable existence
On this little Earth
And as I looked at the stars
I almost lost my breath
When I remembered what great men had said
That I was made from the hearts of dying stars
All of me was not from here, but belonged out
there
And as I closed my eyes
I realised that those twinkling lights
Were not just heavenly bodies
But like an ageing photograph
Were the ghosts of my family
Long since gone.

I SAW ALL OF YOU

I saw you all,
Each one of you trying your best,
Dealing with all the hope and hurt,
Working with all the lost and found.
And I saw all of you,
Making each other laugh and cry,
In a world where no one was sure
When or why, it had occurred.
I saw all of you,
Confused and excited,
loved and hated,
Joking and breaking.
And my time – well my time to leave will soon be nigh,
But I saw something spectacular in all of you.
None of us brought each other here,
But all of us worked at helping other souls through.
I saw all of you, and I cried.
All of you were amazing.

COMING HOME TO YOURSELF

It's cold out there, sometimes,

Perhaps it's just the way the world is,

With all its dark and tiredness and fear,

And you find some days there is nowhere to go,

No one to talk to, no one to listen,

Those are the days when you will come home to
yourself,

Close the door,

And rest –

You are more amazing than you know.

LOST SHOES ON RANNOCH MOOR

The first time I saw them, I thought to myself, 'hello, something up here' and I had these visions of an office worker who had had enough, who had then taken off his shoes and wandered into the wilds of Rannoch Moor. Never to be seen again.

It can be a lonely place, can Rannoch Moor. Full of pools and bogs that can pull a man down and never let him see the sky again.

As the weeks passed, I was amazed that the shoes remained there, I had thought that some wild beast might have a taken them back to their lair or home or whatever, or that some numb skull would have thrown them away.

But there they lay. A little tired and worn, perhaps, but aren't we all?

One Spring day I decided to stop to have a bit of lunch and thought that perhaps the stone table would be a good place to do this.

So I moved the shoes over a little to give me some room, and that was when I noticed the handwritten note pushed down into the toe of the right shoe. I unfurled the paper and read it:

"These are my shoes. Once I was caught on Rannoch Moor with nothing more than my bare feet (it is a long story, don't ask). So these shoes are for you, for whoever needs them. That's what life is about – sharing."

I had to smile, and you know what? I smiled all the way back home.

Life wasn't so bad after all.

SOMEWHERE SAFE

No camera can ever capture
That kindness in your smile
Or the love that's in your eyes
No camera can ever hold
The way I felt as we climbed that hill
Just you and I and the windswept day

No camera can ever show how proud I am of you
How much I love to be with you,
How much I care.
I listen
To the things you say
I feel safe in your presence

And as I turn,
To watch you on this perfect day
I want to hide it all somewhere safe
To play again
When you are no longer here.

THE HOUSE BY THE SEA

There was love above and below me in that house that stood beside the sea.

On clear days I could spot the horizon and that meant everything to me. It was the tallest of houses and the happiest of homes. It was stuffed full to the rafters with sisters and brothers and my mother and father.

We helped each other and we supported each other. We made each other smile and sometimes we made each other cry. Those were the days which were warmed by the sun and seemed to last forever.

In the winter we drank broth and ate stews and hunkered down in the heat of each other's company, comfortable that the others were there. There were card games, singing, communal cooking and laughter, oh yes, the laughter. There was always someone laughing in that house. When the storms hit our home, it rocked and swayed and the more it rocked and swayed, the more we felt safe. Don't ask me what I mean by that, just that you had to be there to understand.

My Grandpa had built it for the simple reason that he wanted to prove you could build a house on the sand by the sea. There were those in town who said he was a brick short of a chimney but my

Grandpa had always believed in himself and so it had happened. And having been built by such a kind soul and even kinder heart meant that the very building seemed to bleed understanding and tolerance.

When it swayed in the wind it sang to us, the building actually felt as if it was telling you that nothing was going to harm you. We were just to relax and bend with the wind.

There was a writing room or rather I used it to write in it, but my brothers and sisters would read, paint, listen to the radio, have heartfelt discussions about the world and all the stars, in it. I learned a lot of things about life in that room and some things I probably shouldn't have.

I realise now how lucky I was back then, what with all that softness, that gentleness, that amount of caring from my family; all of it given to me by some higher force. Boy was I the lucky one. My father and mother taught us to never ever to take anything for granted. To smell the rain, to feel the flowers, to stand on the roof of the house some days and just scream, scream for your very existence. Sometimes I'd scream for the overwhelming energy that was this life and sometimes I would scream for all the injustices that we heap on each other (even on ourselves). There is no crueller person in the world than those things we do to our own minds and hearts. It's like the man said, if we treated other people the way we treated ourselves, we wouldn't last long.

So, I wrote and wrote about the way things changed and the way that things stayed the same. I wrote about love and hate and war and peace.

Those days were the most perfect of my life. But as I've written in these pages before, no one ever tells you that you are passing perfection – you only ever see it in the rear-view mirror and that's when you realise that there's no reverse.

Each morning I could smell the cinnamon wafting its way up the stairs to my room and a few seconds later it was helped along by the smell of the coffee. My mother would be standing at the back porch with the wind coming in off the sea, both hands around her cup of hot brew and deeply breathing in the air.

"Good morning, my much-loved and cherished son," she'd say.
I forgot to mention that my mother came with a warning: she was a crazy as a box of frogs.
"And how has the universe treated you this fine morning?" she'd ask.
"Fine." I'd say – I was trying really hard to cultivate a mysterious air about me at the time given the fact that I intended to be a writer.

"You don't say," then she'd smile, pull her house coat in tight and head back to making the biscuits for breakfast.

Sometimes I would sit with a hand under my chin waiting on the rest of the family to come down, trying to look European (although I wasn't really sure what that meant). Other times I would sit with Grandpa's old pipe and stare out to sea as if the meaning of life was somewhere out there to be found. Man, that pipe tasted really bad.

I went through a spell of chewing tobacco, but it was short-lived due to the vomiting that accompanied it. Then I got a big hat and I decided that was the look for me.

There was a real hot summer when I would wear the hat from first thing in the morning to last thing at night. I even slept with the hat on, but I guess someone would take it off my head when I was fast asleep - while I was dreaming of the future life that I was going to live in that hat.

To be a writer in the last house on the beach was truly the best thing ever, in the whole world. Then one morning my father came into breakfast and told everyone to remain calm and not to worry but Grandma had been taken to hospital. She had been my moon and my stars when I was growing up. She was the one who encouraged me to write, who had read Dickens to me and who now would listen to my own stories.

She'd never say if a story was good or bad, but when she said "My ain't that interesting" I knew it wasn't one of her favourites.

She and my Grandpa lived in the best room at the top of the house, the one with the views and the sunshine, although when my Grandma was there, it always seemed to be full of sunshine.

In the evening when I was writing I could hear the dance music coming from their gramophone. Boy they loved to dance. When they were younger they would travel the county taking part in competitions. Their room was full to the roof with trophies.

When my Grandpa started to get sick neither of them talked about the illness, until the day my Grandpa said that perhaps they shouldn't dance anymore.

The day my Grandma took ill, I went to the hospital in the afternoon, and she was sitting up in bed and smiling. Boy that made me feel a whole lot better.

Every day after school I went straight to the hospital and read her my latest story. At the weekends, if she felt okay, she would read me some of David Copperfield.

In her final week she asked to be allowed home, I didn't know that she was finished, I honestly thought she was getting better.

About two days before she left us for good and while the nurse was downstairs getting a coffee, she asked me to take her up to the roof and to bring the wind-up gramophone, as well.

When we got up there, boy it was warm, and you could see for miles. I turned the handle on the gramophone and put on her favourite tune and then she asked me to dance.

I took her hand and I bowed and then we danced as if she was seventeen again.

I AM SO PROUD OF YOU

I am so proud of you,
In so many ways,
Proud of every sinew in your strained body,
Proud, that with even a fractured heart,
You can still stand and smile,
Still look the world
Straight in the face.

I am so proud of you,
For although you ached for love yourself,
You gave yours away to those who needed it,
Proud that when it took everything inside
Just to get to midday,
You got there and you survived,
And still you remembered and still you cared.

I am so proud of you,
That while you drag all that darkness with you,
You can still make it to the end of the day –
Just please, please remember this,
With all my heart,
I am so proud of you.

THE TIME IT TAKES TO READ THIS STORY

The little book was still there. She'd won it when she was twelve for being best at science in class. When she got older and became a grandmother, she'd passed it on to her granddaughter.

For all the strange life reasons it had been her who had brought her up – not her mother. Now her granddaughter was gone, married and off to the other side of the world. The folks would be here soon to pack the books and furniture.

The little science book would be passed on to her great-grandson or daughter – someone she might never meet.

As she sat still in the room, she knew that nothing could be farther than the truth. No one sat still – not even the dead.

We travelled around the Earth at 1,000 miles an hour, and the Earth travelled around the Sun. And the Sun travelled as the Milky Way moved around in a circle and sped across the Universe.

It was estimated that a person relative to the Universe was travelling at 2.85 million miles an hour – that is 800 miles a second.

In the time it took a person to read a short story, such as this one – you will have travelled about 144,000 miles.

No one stays still.

THE END

Nothing can bring you back. I realise that now, but you'll always live on - inside my head and my heart. x

Printed in Great Britain
by Amazon